THE SCRUFFS

The good, the bad...and the scruffy!

HANNAH SHAW

SCHOLASTIC

Scholastic Children's Books
An imprint of Scholastic Ltd
Euston House, 24 Eversholt Street, London, NW1 1DB, UK
Registered office: Westfield Road, Southam, Warwickshire, CV47 0RA
SCHOLASTIC and associated logos are trademarks and/or
registered trademarks of Scholastic Inc.

First published in the UK by Scholastic Ltd, 2017

ISBN 978 1407 16134 1

A CIP catalogue record for this book
is available from the British Library.

Printed by CPI Group (UK) Ltd, Croydon, CR0 4YY

Papers used by Scholastic Children's Books are made
from wood grown in sustainable forests.

1 3 5 7 9 10 8 6 4 2

www.scholastic.co.uk

For Penny and Gulliver

Chapter One

THE (not so) PERFECT PET

You know the kind of shop you walk past a thousand times and never really notice? The kind of shop that must have been there since your granny was in nappies?

Well, "The Perfect Pet" is that shop. The paint is peeling from the doorframe, the sign is wonky and the posters in the window are faded. If you step a little closer to the entrance, the whiff of musty gerbil poop and damp shavings will tickle your nostrils.

Shall we step inside? *Ting-a-ling!*

What a mess...!

Did you spot?

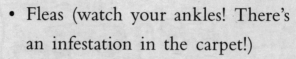

- Fleas (watch your ankles! There's an infestation in the carpet!)
- Rodent bedding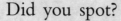
- Dogs' beds
- Birdseed
- Dog biscuits and chews
- Cat scratching posts
- Budgie mirrors
- Grooming brushes
- Collars

Look even harder and you may find the more unusual items such as:

- Meat-flavoured toothpaste (Mmm! Delicious!)

4

- Cat hammocks – for the cat that likes to chill.

- Dog seatbelts – Buckle up, pooches!

- A miniature shipwreck – an essential for a nautical-themed fishtank.

Somewhere asleep at the back of the pet shop is the owner, Mr Straw. He loves all animals (great and small) and would help anything from a grizzly bear to a woodlouse if it was in need.

He spends most of his days dozing, waking only briefly to serve

customers (fortunately for him there aren't very many of those). His jumpers are usually inside out and because he is always losing his glasses, he can't see very much. But this is probably for the best, because if he knew what his beloved pets were up to, he'd be worried...

Pets? I hear you say. *There are pets in here?! Where?*

You can't see them just at the moment because they are playing a game of hide-and-seek.

Shall we go and find them?

Look, over there in the bin of dried peas and sunflower seeds – some ears are poking out. It's **Gerb**! He's a gerbil ... with HUGE ears.

His giant lugholes are very useful and he can hear someone coming from a mile away. He wants to be the first flying gerbil, but he hasn't quite figured that one out yet.

Is that a feather duster? No, it's **Lost** – the budgie. Lost is even more shortsighted than Mr Straw. She only found out her name when she saw herself on a LOST BUDGIE poster. One day she tumbled into the yard of the Perfect Pet shop and she hasn't found her way home since. Lost is now happily "on holiday", as she likes to think of it (secretly, she can't remember where she used to live anyway).

Give a huge round of applause for **Elvis** – the chameleon. Uh-huh! Elvis is an ancient exotic desert chameleon with an exciting musical past (he once belonged to a man who made a living impersonating this really old singer your gran used to like). He has the funky ability to change into loads of colours, unfortunately, he usually ends up picking the wrong one and can't merge into the background. "But having a long, sticky tongue is very handy, thankyouverymuch!"

Grr! Woof! Here comes **Itch!** This lovable flea-ridden mutt has been living in the pet shop the longest and is leader of the pack. He is by far the scruffiest, but he's super-streetwise from years of being a wanderer. He has lost an eye, but he totally rocks the pirate dog look, and his sense of smell is terrific.

And that's all
of the pets that
live in the shop...
Oops, I almost
forgot Slug.

ITCH →

*"What do you
mean? You
forgot about
the BEST
pet here! I'm a
medium-sized garden slug
of immaculate pedigree.
Humph! And I'm the only slug in the world
who can read and write."*

Slug learned to read after eating his
way through the piles of Mr Straw's
newspapers. (And he's not REALLY
a pet ... but don't
tell him that!)

Slug

Together they are the **Scruffs** – the scruffiest, smelliest pets in town!

And no, although this is meant to be a pet *shop*, Mr Straw has no intention of selling *any* of them. This is their home and they love it here.

Together, we are the Scruffs!

Chapter Two

THE PERFECT PET!

It was one of those days where it was too wet to play outside in the yard, so the pets were playing hide-and-seek in the shop.

Itch was the seeker.

Lost was the easiest to find (she had got lost on the way to her hiding place).

Elvis had tried to camouflage himself on a green plant, but had accidentally turned himself sparkly silver.

Gerb was inside a

hamster ball. Itch
could *smell* him a
mile off.

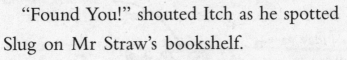

Slug was usually
the hardest to find.
But Itch knew
he had a weakness
for anything made of
paper...

"Found You!" shouted Itch as he spotted
Slug on Mr Straw's bookshelf.

"This one is delicious!" Slug said through
a mouthful of index page. "So many tasty
words."

"That was fun," Itch said, rolling on the
floor and trying to dislodge a particularly
irksome flea.

Ting-a-ling!

"Hello, Itch, my boy!" Mr Straw walked in and gave Itch a good scratch on the tummy.

Mr Straw headed for the counter and carefully put down what he had been carrying. "Now, I have a very special surprise for you all!"

Behold:

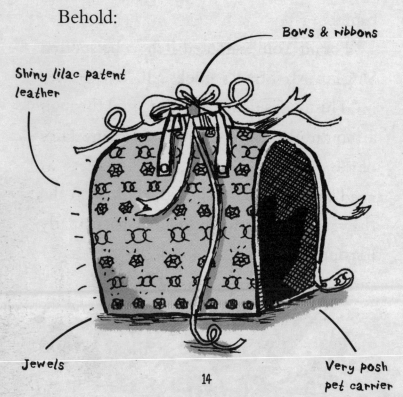

Bows & ribbons

Shiny lilac patent leather

Jewels

Very posh pet carrier

The pets gathered round curiously to look at the lilac-coloured pet carrier Mr Straw had brought with him, which was bejewelled with fabulous gemstones.

"Wow, just look at that!" sighed Elvis longingly. "So much sparkle!"

"It's a tad over the top, if you ask me," snorted Gerb. "What's wrong with a cardboard box with holes in?"

A shadow shifted inside the case.

The pets shuffled back. Something was inside!

Mr Straw unzipped the mesh on the front of the case. "Come on, love," he said. "No need to be shy."

Everyone watched in silence. For a few minutes nothing stirred. Then, out of the case appeared a perfectly manicured paw ...

followed by another ... and then ... the most *beautiful* cat emerged. She was wearing a designer collar that glittered with diamonds and her fur shone like silk.

There was a collective gasp from the gang.

"Everyone, meet Ursula," Mr Straw said. "I'm sure you'll make her feel very at home here." Mr Straw fussed over the cat for a minute before reaching into the carry case and bringing out a purple satin cushion and a pink, fluffy scratching post. "You'll

soon settle in, puss," he said with a smile. "They're a friendly bunch."

Mr Straw made himself a cup of tea and sunk in his chair, and within minutes he had resumed his normal activity: snoring loudly.

Ursula looked around the shop, taking it all in – the dirt, the dust, the grime, the out-of-date kitty snacks. She sniffed and wrinkled up her pink nose.

"Excuse me," she meowed, "but where is your high-definition, extra-large-screen TV? I'm missing *Antiques Roadshow*!"

The Scruffs looked blank. "Errr..." Itch started.

"And can one of you bring me my special food bowl

with my name engraved on it? I usually have some finely-diced salmon around this time, but tuna will do so long as it's fresh."

"Umm..."

"And I can't seem to see a designer sofa with hand-embroidered silk cushions to stretch out on? Is it behind that pile of dented dog-food tins?"

"Well..."

"And surely there must be a roaring birchwood log fire to sit next to somewhere?"

"We don't have any of that here!" burst out Itch. "But we CAN play hide-and-seek, if you like..."

Ursula sighed. "No thank you, that sounds noisy and childish." She sighed again. "I have to admit, I was expecting something a little more high-class. I guess I'll just lie down on my cushion. Perhaps someone will tidy up a bit while I'm asleep."

Itch growled.

WHAT A SNOB! he thought. "Come on, guys! Forget about HER!" he said loudly enough for Ursula to hear. "Lets have fun! Look, the sun has decided to shine!" Indeed the sunlight was now trickling in through the smeary windows.

"Can we play hide-and-seek again?" chirped Lost. "I'm sure I won't get lost this time."

Everyone groaned, but Itch said, "OK, OK, one last game. One … two … three … four…"

Within a minute Itch had found Elvis, Gerb and Slug. But it seemed that Lost really had become good at hiding. Itch couldn't smell her anywhere. Soon everyone was looking for her.

"Is Lost … er … *lost* again?" asked Gerb.

"Are you looking for your feathered friend?" Ursula asked, pointing a claw at the open skylight. "Because the last time I saw her, she was flying out of that window..."

"Oh no!" cried Elvis.

Hide-and-seek had suddenly become real...

Chapter Three

LOST GETS LOST

Of course, Lost hadn't actually meant to fly out of the window. She had tried to hide *near* the window but had somehow managed to fly straight out – and, before she knew it, she was lost again.

Now the budgie was soaring over the town square, flying higher and higher above the shops and houses below.

A flock of pigeons flapped past her.

"Ahoy there, crazy bird!"

A hot-air balloon floated by...

An aeroplane roared past.

Lost was getting tired now. Slowly, slowly, her wings stopped flapping, until. . .

Wheeeeeeeeee!

Down, down, down she fell!

Boing ... boing ... bump! Flump!

Lost rubbed her head and gazed around. She had landed in a delicious-looking cake. The flock of pigeons landed nearby and started teasing her.

"What do you think you are, a racing pigeon?" "I think you need some feather implants" "Tasty landing!"

"Where am I?" Lost asked, but the pigeons just laughed. "How very RUDE!" Lost thought. "I'll go and ask that nice-looking bird over there." She flapped over to where the bird was perched. "Good afternoon! I'm Lost and I'm lost," she said. "I need to find my way back to the Perfect Pet Shop – do you know where it is?"

But the bird didn't reply. It appeared that it did not speak English. Lost tried some of the other languages she knew.

"Err... Das Geschäft fur Haustiere?"

"La boutique pour animaux de compagnie?"

Зоомагазине

ペットショップ

"Y siop anifeiliaid anwes?"

Still no answer. In fact, the bird hadn't even moved. But Lost spoke a lot of languages and wasn't going to give up...

Meanwhile, back in the pet shop, Itch wiped the greasy shop window with his tail and the Scruffs stared out, hoping to  catch a glimpse of the troublesome budgie.

"Wait a minute! I have a sighting!" Itch barked excitedly. "One Lost Budgie, over there by the Cakes-U-Like Cafe! Um ... why is she talking to that lady's hat?"

"LOST!!" The gang jumped up and down and shouted. But Mr Straw had locked the front door and was still fast asleep. There was no way out.

"Why don't we climb through the skylight?" suggested Slug.

"It's too high," groaned Gerb.

"Let's stand on top of each other – that might do it!" cried Itch.

"Nope, this isn't working!" said Slug, straining to reach.

Suddenly… "Oh NO! Look who's a-coming," Elvis gasped, sticking his tongue out in the direction of the tables and chairs.

The Cakes-U-Like Cafe's pet, a big ginger cat called Tom, had strolled out of the shadows and had spotted poor Lost, still perched on a customer's hat. He rubbed himself against the woman's legs till she bent down to stroke him – and then he POUNCED!

Tom Cat missed but Lost tumbled off the brim and got tangled in a ribbon. Dangling desperately in mid-air as Tom swiped at her behind, Lost realized that she was in TROUBLE!

"Yum! Budgie a pinyata," grinned Tom, licking his lips. He jumped up, mouth open, ready to swallow Lost in one gulp...

Chapter Four

Neeeeeoooooowwwww!!!!

Suddenly, a streak of black-and-silver fluff leapt across the pet shop. Using the wobbling tower of Scruffs ("Oof!" That was Slug's head) as a springboard, Ursula dived like a moggie ninja through the open skylight and landed neatly on tiptoe in the street outside.

In a blink she sped off in the direction of the cafe, darting between table legs to the spot where Lost was about to meet her untimely fate. She barged Tom Cat out the way, yelling, "That budgie is MINE!"

Tom Cat cowered and stalked away, muttering threats under his breath. "You'll pay for this! Just you wait and see..."

Ursula ignored him and instead looked at Lost dangling helplessly in mid-air. For a minute she looked as though she quite fancied Lost for a snack herself.

"She's going to eat her!" cried Gerb.

"Man, it's going to get messy!" Elvis groaned. "I'm all shook up!"

"I can't watch!" Slug wailed

"Calm down, everyone," Itch said, but even he couldn't hide his worry.

With one skilful swipe of her razor-sharp claws, Ursula cut the budgie free. Then she graciously lowered her head towards Lost.

"Hop on, little bird! I'll take you back
to the shop."

Luckily, just then Mr Straw woke from
his nap, stretched, yawned and went to
open the front door for some fresh air.
Ursula and Lost slipped in without him

noticing they'd ever left.

The Scruffs rushed to greet them.

"Wow!" breathed Gerb. "You saved her, Ursula!"

"Preeetty impressive," grinned Itch.

Ursula blushed and gently helped Lost off her back. "It was nothing," she said modestly. "It's just I could see you needed help fast, so I stepped in."

"Thanks for saving me, Ursula." Lost was still dazed from her experience but remembered her manners.

"With skills like that, we'd love for you to join our gang," Itch said. "Sorry if we got off on the wrong paw earlier."

Ursula looked stunned for a moment... *Then:*

"That would be amazing!" she cried. "I've never had any animal friends before."

35

"High fives all round! Welcome to the SCRUFFS." Itch panted. "The first rule of the Scruffs is ... er, there are no rules!"

They celebrated with some old dog biscuits. Ursula was soon chatting away.

"I'm sorry if I came across as unfriendly. You see, I've never really met any other animals before. My previous owner was my only friend. She loved me dearly – she even had my portrait painted – but she

never let me out because she didn't want me to get lost. So I was an indoor cat and I wasn't allowed to get dirty, or mess up my fur..." The rest of the Scruffs listened sympathetically as Ursula explained that her rich elderly owner used to groom her every day and lavish her with expensive food and gifts. But as she became too frail to look after Ursula she gave her to her nephew – who hated cats and gave her to Mr Straw.

"All I used to do every day was sit on my cushion in front of the fire watching TV," she sighed. "I know my owner meant well but it did get a little ... dull. I always

37

wondered what it would be like to have friends and fun."

"Well you've come to the right place! And without you Lost could have been ... well, it doesn't bear thinking about!" Gerb exclaimed. "You sure showed that Tom Cat who's boss."

"I'm so sorry for causing so much trouble," Lost sighed. "I just couldn't see where I was going..."

"Hmmm," Ursula said thoughtfully. "Do you have bad eyesight?"

"Bad eyesight?" Slug blurted in. "Lost can't even see her own beak – can you, Lost?"

Lost nodded sadly. "It's true."

"I have an idea," Ursula said. "Hang on a second." She took an old pair of Mr Straw's reading glasses from a shelf, fiddled with the frames for a bit, and then wrapped them around Lost's head. "There we go! Any better?"

"GOSH!" Lost gasped "I can see... I can *see*! It's a miracle."

Ursula held up a mirror. "Look!"

"Oh, what a beautiful bird!" Lost said. "How lovely to meet you."

"No, my dear, that's your REFLECTION," Ursula explained.

Everyone laughed happily as Lost looped the loop around the pet shop, admiring her surroundings as she saw everything properly for the first time. Soon, she was exhausted by the day's excitement and landed on her perch for a nap.

The other animals all grinned at each other. Ursula had saved the day – and shown that she was a proper Scruff after all.

Chapter Five
THE DEN

Whilst Lost snored gently (yes, birds can snore) the other Scruffs were eager to give Ursula "the tour".

"Here's where I sleep," Itch said, pointing to a scratched-up dog bed. "They're meant to be for sale but Mr Straw doesn't sell much so we're free to use whatever we need around the shop." He paused to lick out a tube of extra-meaty toothpaste.

"There are cages

for sale too, but Mr Straw would never lock me in one," Gerb proudly explained.

"And these are our feeding bowls for when it's dinner time," said Itch.

"Most of the day we can just do our own thang," Elvis winked, "because Mr Straw over there is always faaast asleep in his chair."

"Elvis likes to sing karaoke in his spare time, and I'm writing a novel," Slug boasted.

"I'm growing to like it here," Ursula purred. "It's a bit different from what I'm used to, but you guys seem to love it so I'm sure I will too." Ursula put the memory of her previous home – the

42

beautiful apartment with its wall-to-wall carpets, luxurious sofa and high-definition television – to the back of her mind and smiled.

"Small and cosy. It's perfect..."

"Oh, wait a minute – we haven't shown Ursula the most important place!" Itch barked excitedly.

Itch led the way behind Mr Straw's chair, where a doorway led out to a tiny kitchen.

This was where Mr Straw prepared his cups of tea and buttered his cheese-and-pickle sandwiches. Another door with a roomy pet flap led to a walled backyard area.

"You have a garden!" Ursula exclaimed joyfully. "I've heard about gardens but I've never been in one!"

And what a garden – it was more like a jungle. Ursula could see so many exciting places to sharpen her claws, and the air was full of interesting smells.

Itch wagged his tail. "And this is the Den," he said.

THEE DEN
SCRUFFS ONLY—
KEEP OUT.

It looked more like an old rabbit hutch to Ursula, but she was too polite to say so. "Go on in!" said Itch, ushering Ursula inside as the others followed. A few old blankets were draped on the floor and there was a small cupboard nailed to the wall, containing a packet of digestive biscuits stolen from Mr Straw's stash, and an old notebook.

"As our newest member, you can help yourself to the first biscuit," Slug said to Ursula kindly. "Then could you please make your mark in our notebook?"

I hereby declare I am a fully committed member of the Scruffs and I will always help my friends.

Slug.

Ursula cheerfully added her paw print. She was part of the gang now!

"So what do you do in here?" she asked.

"Well, mainly we eat biscuits," Elvis explained.

"But sometimes we do top-secret missions!" chirped Lost, who'd joined them after a refreshing power nap.

"HAHAHAHA!" A peal of laughter echoed from above. The Scruffs stepped outside. In a high branch of a tree sat Tom, the cat from the cafe.

"What a bunch of UGLY misfits," he jeered. "Cat, what possessed you to hang out with those L.O.S.E.R.S – a hairy dog tramp, a rodent dumbo, a crusty old lizard, my lost snack and ... is that a SLUG who thinks he's a pet?"

Ursula hissed angrily. Tom shifted a little uncomfortably even though he was up in the relative safety of the tree.

"You think you can take my pre-dinner appetiser off me and get away with it?" he hissed back. "Well, just you wait. I'm watching you all in your stupid secret den, probably making stupid plans… I'll get my revenge."

"Buzz off!" growled Itch. He hated that cat.

"Ah, let's ignore him." Ursula smiled and flicked her tail, strolling casually back through the pet flap and flopping down in her new dusty basket. She was blissfully weary … this might just have been the most exciting day of her life.

Ting-a-ling!

Ursula woke up. The morning sun was bright outside the pet-shop window.

But wait... What was this? Customers? The animals all gasped in astonishment – it had been months since an actual real-life customer had been seen inside the shop. Mr Straw was surprised too. He leapt to his feet and straightened his back-to-front jumper, accidentally knocking his breakfast tea all over his newspaper and narrowly missing Slug, who was reading the small ads.

"Um... Welcome to the P-P-P-Perfect Pet Shop. I'm Mr Straw. Are you after anything in particular?"

"He's putting on the proper shop-owner act," giggled Gerb.

"Shh!" Lost squawked, peering through her new glasses. "I don't like the

50

look of these customers..."

Indeed, the customers were not the usual type. The few people who – very rarely – came to the Perfect Pet Shop were usually pretty scruffy themselves. These customers were very smart. They looked clean and shiny. The lady seemed to recoil as Mr Straw bumbled towards them, and the little girl scrunched up her nose.

"Mummy, it SMELLS awful in here..."

"What ... what are those?" the woman asked, looking aghast as she stared at each one of the Scruffs in turn.

"Oh, they're my lovely animals," Mr Straw said, smiling proudly. "Now, how can I help you?" The lady backed away even further, almost sticking her heel into poor Slug, who had slid over eagerly to greet them.

"Eeeeek!" shrieked the lady. "A slug! Disgusting! I hope it didn't get slime on my shoe."

Slug turned a bright shade of pink. His feelings were terribly hurt, and he slid off to a dark corner.

"Come on, Bunty," snapped the woman. "This is a mistake — there are clearly no pets for you here. We're leaving."

But Bunty was staring at Ursula and her little face had lit up.

Mummy! Look at that lovely cat! She can be my pet!

"No, Bunty! I told you, we're leaving right now."

Bunty screwed up her face and began to shriek. "But, Mummy! I WANT THAT CAT!"

The noise was ear-splitting. Poor Mr Straw covered his ears in shock, Itch covered his with his paws, Lost squawked in terror, and Gerb, whose hearing was sensitive at the best of times, stuck his head in a pile of shavings.

The woman sighed. "Fine. I suppose we can have her fumigated." She took out her purse from her handbag. "How much for the cat?"

Bunty stopped shrieking and Mr Straw rubbed his head in astonishment.

"Err, that cat isn't for sale. She only just arrived yesterday and I..."

The woman shoved a wad of crisp notes into Mr Straw's hand and said, in a voice that oozed venom, "I suggest you reconsider. What my little princess wants, my little princess gets."

There was a moment where all the animals held their breath, and then Mr Straw looked at the floor. He was clearly no match for the customer's steely gaze. "I – I need time to get her tidied up a bit," he muttered. "But

you can have her tomorrow."

Bunty's pout turned into a huge grin.
"I looooove you, MUMMYKINS!" she
sang in the most sickening way. Then she
shrieked again, this time with delight,
and ran over to Ursula,
picking her up
around the middle
and squeezing her
far too tightly.
Ursula struggled
to breathe.

"Bunty!" said
her mother. "We
will collect the
cat tomorrow." She
gave Mr Straw a hard
stare. "When she has been de-fleaed and
wormed."

And with that the woman took hold of

Bunty's hand and dragged her out the shop, slamming the door behind her.

Mr Straw slumped down into his chair and put his head in his hands. The animals were all speechless. Ursula couldn't believe what had just happened – but one thing was for sure, she did not want to be a pet to THAT dreadful family.

Chapter Six

OPERATION: SAVE URSULA!

Mr Straw was still shaking his head and muttering long after the woman and the little girl had left. He kept staring at the notes in his hand. The animals could tell that, while he didn't want to part with Ursula, he had never seen so much money.

"I don't think we can rely on Mr Straw to help us on this one," Itch said worriedly. "He doesn't know what to do. Ursula's future is in DANGER. We need to call a SCRUFFS meeting RIGHT NOW."

Itch grabbed a dog whistle from the shelf and blew hard. *Pheeep!*

"Would all Scruffs make their way outside to the Den, please? It's an EMERGENCY."

The animals crowded
into the hutch,
all talking
at once.
"I can't
believe
it ... the
cheek!" said Lost.

"There's no time to lose – they'll be back tomorrow," said Gerb.

"She almost trod on me," said Slug.

"I don't think they knew the first thing about cats ... or animals, for that matter," said Itch.

"Oh, lordy!" said Elvis

"What are we going to dooooo," wailed Slug.

"WOULD EVERYONE JUST BE QUIET?" Ursula yelled above the din. Everyone fell silent. "Look, there's no time to talk – we need action. I don't want to go back to being anyone's pet; I want to stay here and be one of the gang and have lots of fun adventures. And can you imagine what life will be like with those two?"

Everyone thought for a moment.

There would be lots of CUDDLES...

There would almost certainly be HAIRDRESSING...

And lots of WALKS...

Not to mention DRESSING UP...

"...and then they'll go away on holiday and forget to feed me," Ursula mewed sadly. She'd never had a day in her life when she hadn't eaten well. The horror of it all. She put her head in her paws.

"Ursula's right," said Elvis. "We need to stop jib-jabbering and help this kitty!" Slug got out the notebook and sharpened the pencil. "Right. Everyone suggest an idea to stop Ursula being taken away and we'll go with the best one."

Slug: She could make herself invisible? Problem: HOW exactly?!

Gerb's Idea: Ursula disguises herself as a chicken. Problem: Might not be very convincing.

Itch's Idea: She could run away tonight... Problem: But where would she go?

Then Elvis, who'd been staring into the distance all the while, said in a long slow drawl... "What she needs is ... a make-under!"

"A *make-under*? Why ... why ... that's it! Elvis, you're a *genius*!" Itch laughed.

Elvis changed colour to a light pink tone. "Thankyouverymuch, hound dog!"

All the other Scruffs looked puzzled. "We don't get it," said Lost.

"Think about it," Itch said. "Why did Ursula get picked today instead of one of us? In fact, can any of you remember anyone EVER wanting to buy one of us?"

The animals all shook their heads and Itch carried on.

"Why? Well, Ursula is a primped and preened pedigree cat with perfect silky fur and we're … well … scruffy, dirty and smelly. We need to make Ursula more *Scruff*! What do you think, Ursula?"

Ursula thought for a minute and then grinned. "That's the smartest … erm … *scruffiest* idea I've ever heard. Do your worst, guys!"

"Yee-ha! It's time to get scruffy!"

Chapter Seven
LET'S GET SCRUFFY!

"Stay still, Ursula, I haven't finished yet," Slug protested.

"But it tickles," Ursula giggled. "And this is taking ages."

The yard was a hive of activity as all the Scruffs set to work giving Ursula the make-under of a lifetime.

"It takes time to slime," Slug tutted, frowning in concentration. He had been busy covering Ursula from head to tail in slug slime goo-trails. Elvis was holding up a mirror to show Ursula her make-under progress.

Meanwhile Lost was perched on Ursula's

head, combing her fur backwards in little clumps with her claws.

"Good back-combing, Lost!" Elvis was impressed. Slug's slime acted like super-strength hair gel and her fur now stuck out in all directions.

"We're getting there!" Ursula chirped.

Gerb had collected shavings from an old bag of bedding and put them in a pile.

"If you're finished," he said, "roll in this!"

Ursula had never rolled in anything before! Tentatively she lay down and wiggled a bit.

"No! No! Like this!" Itch explained, flopping down on the ground and wiggling frenziedly on his back.

Ursula tried again, "Ooh! This is fun!" Soon sawdust had stuck to all the slime in her matted fur.

"How do I look?" she said breathlessly, looking round at all the Scruffs.

They stared at her for a moment and then everyone burst out laughing!

"What?" she said, hurt. "Hasn't it worked?"

"Oh, it's worked," gasped Itch, when he could speak. "You look absolutely terrible! It's brilliant – no one will want to take you home like that!"

"Really? Thanks, gang!" Ursula was really pleased. "But this sawdust is itchy. I don't think I'll be keeping this hairstyle for long..."

Just then, Mr Straw's voice called out across the yard. "Come and get your dinner!"

The animals grinned at each other. They had done a

fantastic job of turning Ursula into a real Scruff. NO ONE would want to buy her now!

Back in the shop. Mr Straw, still looking worried, was dishing out the animal's dinners. There were crickets for Elvis, some dried peas for Gerb, a sesame stick for Lost, a large plate of roast chicken and dog biscuits for Itch. There was nothing for Slug, but he was quite happy finishing off everyone's leftovers. For pudding he munched through the sports section of the local paper.

As Mr Straw bent down to give Ursula a plate of succulent pilchards he stumbled backwards in surprise. He took his glasses off, cleaned them and then put them back on again.

"What?! Wait a minute? What's happened to you, puss? Oh dearie me, you weren't like that this morning! You need a BATH."

A *BATH*? Ursula bristled. Like all cats she simply HATED BATHS. She started to run for the yard, but Mr Straw scooped her up and headed for the kitchen sink.

Oh no! All the effort the Scruffs had put into her amazing make-under would be washed away!

Mr Straw got out a bottle of pink pet-wash from a cupboard and soon bubbles were frothing in the bowl. Ursula meowed and hissed and spat but it was no use. Gently but firmly, Mr Straw lowered her into the sink.

"Nooooo!" Itch rushed over, howling in protest and Mr Straw looked at him in surprise.

"Feeling left out? Do you want a bath too, lad? Actually, you could do with a wash..."

And to Itch's horror, the next minute he had joined Ursula in the sink.

71

Soon the reluctant pets were scrubbed clean. The kitchen was now awash with puddles and bubbles and in the middle of it all Itch and Ursula dripped miserably as Mr Straw cheerily towel dried them.

It wasn't long before Ursula was looking beautiful again. Her fur gleamed as Mr Straw combed it back to how it had been. (Itch didn't look much different apart from his eyepatch, which was wonky, and his fur, which was super fluffy like a baby lamb.)

"There you go – looking lovely!" said Mr Straw, giving them both a pat. "Well, night-night, gang. And Ursula, I'm sorry that you're being collected tomorrow – but, er, they seem like lovely people..." His voice trailed off and he sighed, then turned the lights off and went upstairs to bed.

Ursula was too miserable to speak. She knew she'd stand no chance of escaping now.

The Scruffs sat in silence in their beds and a gloom hung over the room.

Itch, however, was deep in thought. "Don't fret, Ursula," he reassured her. "Gather round, everybody. I have Another Plan."

The Perfect Pet Shop was supposed to open at nine, but Mr Straw was famous for over-sleeping, so he set his alarm clock every night. But the next morning when he opened his eyes he saw to his horror that it was past eleven o'clock!

That MIGHT have had something to do with the Scruffs...

ANOTHER PLAN:

7:00 a.m.

Gerb sneaks into Mr Straw's bedroom and turns off the alarm clock.

8:00 a.m.

Itch steals the shop door keys (and a couple of tasty dog biscuits) from Mr Straw's coat pocket.

8:10 a.m.

Lost unlocks the door (with help from Elvis and Ursula).

8:30 a.m.

All Scruffs leave the shop ready for Part Two of the plan.

Chapter Eight
THE PARK

"Attention, gang!" Itch said as the Scruffs blinked in the daylight. "I know the street is full of exciting smells but we need to stay focused. The most important thing is to make Ursula grubby again... Now let's think – where can we go to get her *really* dirty?"

"Look!" cried Elvis as he spotted a whole group of children walking with their parents on the

opposite side of the road. They were all wearing wellington boots and heading in the same direction.

"Follow them!" barked Itch "Where there are children, dirt is *never* far behind!"

Off they went. Itch led the way with Elvis hanging off his collar and Lost flapped above him like a budgie balloon, a piece of string connecting them (to prevent her flying off again) with Gerb riding on her back for a better view. Ursula trotted silently behind with Slug riding on the end of her tail. The animals were all silent — their mission was too important for chatter. They needed to make Ursula as disgusting as possible, and there was no time to lose.

At the Cakes-U-Like Cafe, Tom Cat was bored. He was half-dozing on top of a pile of brioche buns in the shop window, peering out at the world going by...

Just another boring sort-of morning... Children off to the park again...

Wait a second? What's this? "Where are those silly pets off to?" He leapt up. "And what *are* they up to?" He pressed his face to the glass as they disappeared around the corner...

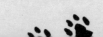

The group of children were so busy chattering amongst themselves that it wasn't until they got to the big gates — where a sign read WELCOME TO THE PARK — ALL PETS MUST BE KEPT ON LEADS — that they noticed they were being followed. Their jaws dropped as Itch, Elvis, Lost, Gerb, Ursula and Slug strolled casually past them. The children started whispering.

Is that a gerbil with ENORMOUS ears?

Is that budgie wearing glasses?

Does that dog have an eyepatch?

And is that a chameleon riding on the dog?!

A sausage dog and a miniature poodle barked in astonishment. "What a rag-tag bunch of odd-balls," said one to the other. "Ha ha ha!! Just look at them!" They laughed so hard they tied themselves in knots.

Even the squirrels in the trees were sniggering.

"I don't really understand why everyone is laughing," Ursula said. "I'm not even scruffy yet..."

"They are just jealous of our unique qualities," Gerb said firmly.

"Look!" said Itch. "The playground!"

It was the best playground in town. There was a slide with a great big muddy patch at the bottom, a dozen swings, a great roundabout, some see-saws and a zip-line with a dirty pile of bark chippings underneath. There was even a grubby tunnel to crawl through and as many big splashy puddles as you could count. It was PERFECT.

"Off you go, Ursula," said Itch. "You need to get as dirty as possible".

"We want to play too!" cried the other

Scruffs, and soon they were whizzing down
the slide, rolling in the bark chippings and

dashing back and forth through the tunnel.

The children in the playground screeched with excitement as the Scruffs ran through puddles, spraying muddy water everywhere. Soon everyone was filthy.

Ursula even managed to get an old sock stuck on her tail. When they had finished, the Scruffs all agreed that this had been the Best Fun Ever. "Even better than playing hide-and-seek," agreed Lost.

"Well I do have the greatest ideas," Itch boasted happily. "But Ursula, all that mud could be easily washed off – we can't make that mistake again. We need to do more..."

"Leaves!" squeaked Gerb. Neat piles of

leaves that had been raked that morning by
the park-keeper were just waiting there ...
for a...

"Leaf fight!" yelled Itch. Soon leaves and
twigs and catkins were stuck in Ursula's
muddy fur as the Scruffs threw leaves at
each other and rolled around like puppies.
They were all out of breath when Elvis

(who had turned purple in the brown leaves) spotted: "Ice cream! Sweet and sticky and PERFECT for our needs."

An ice-cream van had just parked up on the grass and a queue was starting to form. Parents and children leapt away from the muddy animals as they barged their way in through a crowd of legs. Ursula was closest to the front of the queue. "Stand there!" Itch hissed.

A toddler was just being handed a huge melting ice cream. "That's the one! Now – wait for it ... GO!" Itch nudged Ursula forwards and she wrapped herself around the toddler's legs. "Puddy!" squealed the toddler delightedly.

SPLAT! The toddler dropped her ice cream on Ursula's back. **"Waaah!"**

RESULT!

The Scuffs lolled around on the green grass in the sunshine and waited for Ursula's new sticky ice-cream coat to dry. Soon it was rock hard. However hard Mr Straw tried now, he'd never get the combination of mud, leaves and ice cream glue out of her fur in time.

"Oi, you pesky vermin! Was it you messing up my leaves?" a loud voice shouted, disturbing the peace.

The Scruffs leapt to their feet. A grumpy man in a park-keeper's jacket wielding a rake was looming over them. "I'm going to teach you a lesson you won't

forget!" he shouted.

The gang looked at each other and
the crowd of annoyed adults and amused
children, squirrels and pets who had
gathered to goggle.

"Well, what are we waiting for?" Ursula
hissed urgently. **"RUN!"**

Chapter Nine

A PERFECT PONG

Tom Cat was still in the cafe window, washing his paws and waiting for the Scruffs to come back, when...

Zooom!

He blinked.

Was that those scruffy pets? They'd gone so fast he couldn't be sure. Then...

Zip!

A red-faced man with a rake sped past. Was this a chase?

This was too exciting. Tom Cat leapt down from his window sill and dashed out

of the cat-flap, hurrying along the street
after the man.

"The park-keeper is still behind us!" Gerb yelled to Itch. "But if we turn right down that alley we'll lose him!" Itch veered down the alley and Ursula followed. They both stood still, their backs to the wall. Lost almost missed the turning, stumbled, and did a slow-motion (crash) landing on to the cobbles. Gerb rolled off her back, landing in a heap against the wall.

To their relief, they saw the park-keeper running past the entrance to the alley, and then a few minutes later he walked past again, heading back towards the park, looking puzzled and puffed out.

"I think he's given up," Gerb said, pricking up his ears. "Phew."

Itch stopped panting and sniffed the air. . .

"Poooooeeey!"

The others looked at Itch, baffled.

"Can't anyone else smell that?"

"Uh? What?"

Itch trotted down the alley, following his nose. He stopped by some bins and called for the others to come and smell. "Ergh, that is PONGY!" agreed Slug. "Even for us!"

"Where's it coming from?" asked Gerb. "We need stinky smells right now!"

A couple of rats were gnawing on a bone in the corner. "Let's go and ask them," Itch said.

"Can we help you?" they asked suspiciously.

"We are the Scruffs," Gerb explained.

"And we're on an important mission," continued Itch. "A little girl wants to buy our friend, so we need to make her as scruffy and yucky as possible..." He introduced them to Ursula. The rats listened politely (all rats are polite, unlike pigeons).

"Well, she's QUITE scruffy now," said the

first rat. "But there's just one problem..."

"She smells just like ice-cream," said the second rat. "And what do *all* children like?"

"ICE-CREAM."

"Our advice is to jump in those bins over there!" The rats pointed. "That's where that smell is coming from. Then you'll stink just like us!"

Ursula looked at the leaky bins, overflowing with putrid rubbish, and her nose wrinkled. She hadn't minded rolling in sawdust, or leaves, or mud, but surely bin juice was a step too far?

"Come on, it's not that bad!" said Itch. "I used to sleep in bins when I was young pup." *Although none quite as smelly as this*, he thought to himself. To demonstrate, he climbed into a bin, which was lying on its side, and lounged in the rubbish, wagging his tail. The others decided to show Ursula it wasn't so bad either, so they all joined in.

Eventually, screwing up her nose, Ursula went in. The smell was awful as she rolled around in mouldy banana skins, half-empty bean cans, greasy fish bones, rotten cabbage and out-of-date eggs.

"OK, enough already!" Ursula cried, and she waded out.

"How do we smell, rats?" Gerb asked.

The rats sniffed. "You stink divine! We think you smell great – which means you smell awful..."

Everyone thanked them for their help and agreed that rats were indeed very polite and helpful creatures.

"Right, I think Part Two of the plan has been a success. Now it's time to get back to the shop, so that Ursula can be rejected – that way she gets to stay, and Mr Straw won't get into trouble with the customers." Itch herded the gang back towards the entrance of the alley.

"Not so fast, Scruffs," came a sneering voice. "You'll have to get past me first." There was Tom Cat, and he was blocking their way out. "I know you're up to something. What is it?"

"None of your business! Now get out of our way," Ursula glowered.

"*JUST LOOK AT YOU!*" Tom Cat howled with laughter and pointed at her. "What have you done to yourself? You look TERRIBLE!"

"Do I?" Ursula smiled. "Oh, good."

This was not the reaction Tom Cat was expecting. He was used to being annoying. He stepped a little closer and tried another insult. "You are one U.G.L.Y. cat," he said, putting his paw to his nose. "Oh..." He started to turn a little green. "You smell..."

The Scruffs crowded around Tom Cat, trying to stink him out.

"Oh ... you smell REVOLTING! But why? Why would you want to smell like that?"

His eyes narrowed. "I don't know what your plans are but when I saw you leave this morning you certainly didn't look like you do now – especially not you, my fine cat. My guess would be Mr Straw finally

97

wants to sell a pet and you lot don't want him to." Tom Cat started to chuckle. "I'm going to make sure you don't get away with this. Just wait while I go and tell Mr Straw what you're up to." With that, he turned and sped away.

"Phew!" cried Lost. "He's gone."

"No, Lost, you don't understand," groaned Itch. "If he wakes up Mr Straw before we let ourselves back in the shop, he'll know we've escaped and he'll have time to give

us a bath. We need to get back before that Tom Cat does and we can lock him out!"

"We need transport! What about if we all get in that!?" Gerb said, pointing to an abandoned shopping trolley.

The pets all sped past, much to Tom's horror. "Grr! You cheats!"

The filthy, stinky Scruffs reached the door of the Perfect Pet Shop. They let themselves inside as quietly as they could, and crept into their beds.

Eventually, they heard the Town Hall bell chime for eleven o'clock, followed by the familiar shuffle of Mr Straw's slippers coming downstairs.

Mr Straw scratched his head when he saw the time on the shop clock. "How on earth..." he yawned. "I must have slept in." Then... "Odd smell in here..." Luckily he barely glanced at the Scruffs as he was still half-asleep and hadn't made himself his first morning cup of tea yet. (Without his morning cup of tea, Mr Straw did not function properly). He pottered off to the kitchen.

Ting-a-ling!

IT WAS THE CUSTOMERS! The animals all gulped in excitement. Time to see if their plan would work...

Still confused, Mr Straw stumbled to the front door and let in the customers from the day before.

"Eww," the woman said. "It smells VERY odd in here. Even compared to yesterday. Excuse me – are you wearing pyjamas?"

"Er, come in," said Mr Straw, scratching blearily at his face. "Usually I'm dressed by this time, but my alarm clock must have malfunctioned..."

The woman rolled her eyes. "It doesn't matter. We're in hurry. We've come for the cat!"

Bunty, who was sucking on a lollipop, said nothing, but her arms were folded and her eyes were glaring and she tapped her foot impatiently.

"I ... err..." Mr Straw's face was white with misery. He clearly did not want to give Ursula away.

"Chop-chop. I expected you to have her ready. After all, I did give you a very generous deposit yesterday..."

"Err..."

"Well, what's her name?" the woman demanded. "I'll call her myself."

"Err ... it's Ursula."

"URRRRSULA!" The woman screeched.

Bunty took the lolly out of her mouth and pointed to the corner of the shop where the food products were stored. Ursula's tail was sticking out behind a stack of tins.

"Mummy, she's over there!"

"Finally." The woman strode over, grabbed Ursula by the tail, and dragged her out.

"Neeeeow!" Ursula protested.

"Here's the ickle pussycat you wanted, my princess..." she began, ready to hand her over to the girl.

"Meow?"

"AGGGgggHhhh!"
The woman took one look at the cat she was holding and dropped her. Ursula landed at Bunty's feet and stared up at their horrified faces.

"Meeeow!?" She tried again (she was starting to enjoy this!).

"EEEEK! Mummy! That's not the same cat, just look at it!"

"JUST SMELL IT!" The woman grabbed a hankie to her face and realized her hands were covered in stinky, sticky guck. "Agghhhhhh!" she cried again.

"MUUUUMMMMMMMMMY!" yelled Bunty. "It's NOT FAIR! I HATE YOU! I want another PET, NOW NOW NOW!" and she threw herself on the floor and pounded her fists.

The woman tried to compose herself but she was not coping. "Bunty, get up!" But Bunty continued to kick and yell and cry.

"Surely there are other pets in here?" she hissed desperately at Mr Straw. "One that is not quite as hideous as this one?"

"Yes, there are other animals, but they are not for sale," said Mr Straw, who had been watching in amazement. "You already met them yesterday ... come out, folks," he called softly.

The Scruffs rushed out from their hiding places and they all made sure they got a little too close to the awful customers. Itch made himself lick the woman (even though she tasted of strong perfume, which wasn't very nice).

"Oh, NOT them!" The woman started to wail. "Get them away!"

It was too much: the pong of the Scruffs, their filthy coats, scales, feathers – *and* that slug! Not to mention the useless pet shop owner and her tantruming daughter. The woman began to look faint; she stumbled and fell against the rack of fish tanks. The shelf wobbled, and a whole tank of green water full of slimy pond weed (but luckily, no fish) tipped over on top of her head, soaking her from head to toe. This was followed by a gentle rain of red fish food flakes, which stuck all over her.

The shock of seeing this happen to her mother made Bunty stop crying, and instead she started laughing. She laughed so much that the Scruffs and Mr Straw started laughing too.

It was at that moment that Tom Cat burst through the door, panting and desperate to get the Scruffs into trouble.

"Mummy, LOOK! That's the cat I want!" Bunty had stopped laughing and was pointing eagerly at Tom Cat, who looked confused. He started to back away, but it was too late – Bunty grabbed him and hugged him so tight his eyes began to water.

"Oh, that one isn't mine..." Mr Straw began.

"No, that's because he's MINE!" squeaked Bunty cheerily. She stuck her lolly back in her mouth, took hold of her dripping-

wet mother's hand and led her out of the shop.

"Bye!" she said in a sing-song voice. "Thanks for the cat. We probably won't be back."

The Scruffs watched in wonder as Tom Cat was carried away, helpless in the little girl's iron grip.

"Well," Mr Straw said, finally. "I don't know what happened here this morning, but it's all worked out for the best." Ursula gave his leg an affectionate rub. "Phew! The only thing I DO know is that you are all having a bath — starting with you..."

Chapter Ten

A CLOSE SHAVE

"Did you see Tom Cat's face as that little girl pounced? I'll never forget it!" Itch chuckled, yawned and adjusted his eyepatch. He stretched out leisurely in the back yard. "And I've *never* had to endure two baths in one week."

"I just got away with a brush of Mr Straw's toothbrush," boasted Gerb. "Baths and gerbils don't mix."

"I got a shower," said Elvis, "with the plant spray! Uh-huh!"

Lost wasn't saying much; she was too busy flapping her wings to try and dry them off. She didn't like being damp and all that warm water had steamed her glasses up.

Slug had given himself a wash with the watering can. He had started to feel a little dried up and crispy with all the mud clogging his pores.

They all turned and gasped when Ursula stepped out of the cat flap.

Poor Ursula – the mud +leaves +ice cream + bin juice combination had matted her fur into a tangle of dreadlocks that just wouldn't come out, however hard Mr Straw tried. In the end he'd borrowed a pair of clippers from the barber's opposite. His hairdressing skills left much to be desired.

"How did you like your … erm … close shave?" Itch asked Ursula. He chuckled a little.

"That's quite a different look for you,

Ursula," cackled Gerb.

Ursula rolled her eyes. "It's much cooler without all that fur."

"Don't worry, Ursula," Lost tried to reassure her. "I'm sure it will grow back one day."

The funny thing was, it never did! Not

that Ursula minded; she was a fully-fledged Scruff now and she most certainly looked the part.

"It's unlikely anyone will *ever* want me as a pet looking like this," she mewed. "And I couldn't be happier!"

"We're not pets," said Itch. "We're Mr Straw's animal friends, and that's the way we'll stay! Hurrah for the Scruffs!"

"Viva los Scruffs!" echoed Elvis.

"If we're not pets then that means we won't be able to enter the local Pet Show, will we?" laughed Slug, showing the gang an advert he'd found in Mr Straw's newspaper.

"Well, I wouldn't mind all that money," said Itch...

"Shall we enter?" gasped Gerb. "Do you think we could win?"

ADVERTISMENT

TOWN NEWS MAY 20

IS your Pet BEAUTIFUL STYLISH or CLEVER?

Enter the town fete and

PET SHOW
at the playing field

TOP PRIZE winners go to

The most Prestigious Pet Show in the country with a chance to win £100,000!!!

"Maybe," said Ursula, looking determined, "what we need is a special Scruffs plan..."

Hannah Shaw is an award-winning author and illustrator of young fiction and picture books. Her books include Stan Stinky, Sewer Hero and Stan Stinky vs the Sewer Pirates as well as Bear on a Bike and School for Bandits. Hannah's illustrations can be seen in books by other authors such as Gareth Edwards' The Disgusting Sandwich and the Sophie stories by Dick King-Smith. She lives on the outskirts of a friendly Cotswold town with her scruffy family and her old smelly dog. She has at least eight unofficial pet slugs who like to glide around her kitchen at night.

Also available by Hannah Shaw...

Meet Stan Stinky – the unluckiest rat in the sewer. But when UNCLE RATTS and his sidekick, ROACHY the cockroach, disappear, Stan must become an ADVENTURER, SURFER and SEWER HERO to save them!

Stan Stinky wants to be a DETECTIVE, but
the sewers are crime-free. Until … PIRATES
arrive and steal the town's treasures! Can Stan
solve the mystery before it's TOO LATE?

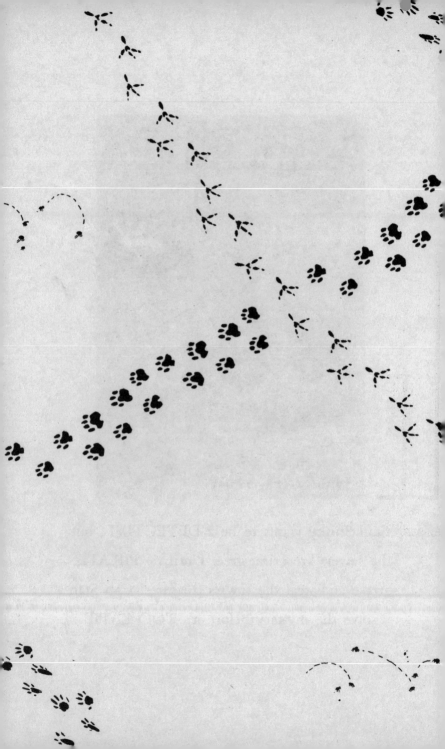